The Anteater's Tongue

Written by Jill Eggleton
Illustrated by Fraser Williamson

Rigby

The anteater is looking for lunch.

He can see ants!

The ants can see the anteater.

2

3

Some ants go
in the log.

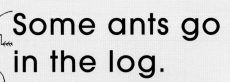

Some ants go
under the leaf.

But some ants stay
in the grass.

The anteater can see
the ants in the grass.

His tongue comes out.
Zap!

No ants are in the grass!

7

The anteater can see
the ants under the leaf.

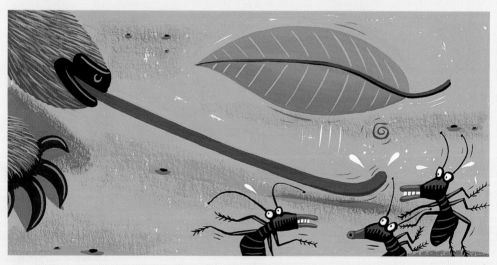

His tongue comes out.
Zap!

No ants are under the leaf!

The anteater
looks in the log.

His tongue
comes out.

Oops!
His tongue is **stuck**
in the log!

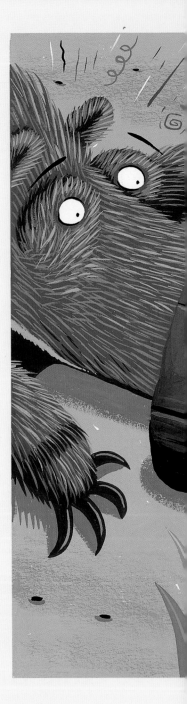

The anteater cannot get
his tongue out.

But the ants are not staying
to help.

The ants get out of the log.
They go up the tree!

The anteater will get
his tongue out.
But the ants are safe.

A Story Sequence

1
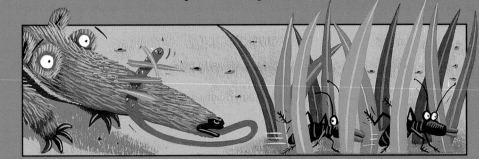

2
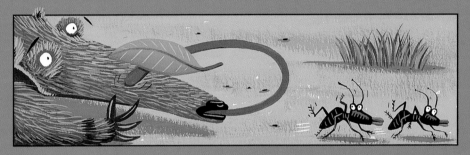

3

4

Guide Notes

Title: The Anteater's Tongue
Stage: Early (2) – Yellow

Genre: Fiction
Approach: Guided Reading
Processes: Thinking Critically, Exploring Language, Processing Information
Written and Visual Focus: Story Sequence
Word Count: 132

THINKING CRITICALLY
(sample questions)
- What do you think this story could be about?
- Focus on the title and discuss.
- How do you know the anteater's tongue is good for getting ants?
- Why do you think the log was a good place for the ants to hide?
- Where else do you think the ants could have gone to get away from the anteater?
- How do you think the anteater will get his tongue out of the log?

EXPLORING LANGUAGE

Terminology
Title, cover, illustrations, author, illustrator

Vocabulary
Interest words: anteater, tongue, log, grass, leaf, zap, oops, stuck
High-frequency words: stay, some, looks
Positional words: out, under, in, up

Print Conventions
Capital letter for sentence beginnings, periods, commas, exclamation marks